The Ladybird Key Words Reading Scheme is based on these commonly used words. Those used most often in the English language are introduced first—with other words of popular appeal to children. All the Key Words list is covered in the early books, and the later titles use further word lists to develop full reading fluency. The total number of different words which will be learned in the complete reading scheme is nearly two thousand. The gradual introduction of these words, frequent repetition and complete 'carry-over' from book to book, will ensure rapid learning.

The full colour illustrations have been designed to create a desirable attitude towards learning — by making every child *eager* to read each title. Thus this attractive reading scheme embraces not only the latest findings in word frequency, but also the natural interests and activities of happy children.

Each book contains a list of the new words introduced.

W MURRAY, the author of the Ladybird Key Words Reading Scheme, is an experienced headmaster, author and lecturer on the teaching of reading. He is co-author, with J McNally, of Key Words to Literacy — *a teacher's book published by The Teacher Publishing Co Ltd.*

THE LADYBIRD KEY WORDS READING SCHEME has 12 graded books in each of its three series—'a', 'b' and 'c'. These 36 graded books are all written on a controlled vocabulary, and take the learner from the earliest stages of reading to reading fluency.

The 'a' series gradually introduces and repeats new words. The parallel 'b' series gives the needed further repetition of these words at each stage, but in a different context and with different illustrations.

The 'c' series is also parallel to the 'a' series, and supplies the necessary link with writing and phonic training.

An illustrated booklet—*Notes for using the Ladybird Key Words Reading Scheme*—can be obtained free from the publishers. This booklet fully explains the Key Words principle. It also includes information on the reading books, work books and apparatus available, and such details as the vocabulary loading and reading ages of all books.

Published by Ladybird Books Ltd Loughborough Leicestershire UK
Ladybird Books Inc Lewiston Maine 04240 USA

BOOK 2a
The Ladybird Key Words Reading Scheme

We have fun

by W MURRAY
with illustrations
by HARRY WINGFIELD

Ladybird Books

Here is Peter
and here is Jane.

Here is Pat, the dog.

new word

Pat

Peter is here.

Jane is here
and Pat is here.

Here they are.

new words

they   are

Here they are
in the water.

They like the water.

Pat likes the water.

Pat likes fun.

---

new words

water   fun

Come in, Pat.

It is fun.

It is fun in the water.

Come in the water.

Come, come, come.

---

new words

come It it

Pat comes in.

Pat likes the water.

It is fun in the water, says Peter.

---

new word

says

I have a ball, says Peter.

Here is the ball.

Here is the ball, Pat,
he says.

---

new words

have   he

Look, look, says Jane.

Look, Peter, look.

Have a look.

Come and look.

Peter has a look.

---

new word

Look   look

Peter looks.

A fish, says Jane.

It is a fish, says Peter.

It is a fish, he says.

---

new word

fish

Look, says Peter.

The dog wants the fish.

He wants the fish, Jane.

---

new word

wants

Pat wants the fish.

No, no, no, says Jane,
you come here.

Come here, Pat, come here.

No, no, no.

---

new words

No   no   you

Here are Peter and Jane.

Peter has some water.

Here you are, Jane,
he says.

---

new word

some

Here you are, Jane,
says Peter.

Here you are.

This is for you.

Here is some water
for you.

new words

for   This   this

This is for you, Jane says.

Here is some water
for you.

Here you are, Peter.

It is for you.

Look Jane, I can jump,
says Peter.

I can jump in the water.

Can you jump
like this, Jane?

new words

can   jump

Jane can jump
and Peter can jump.

They jump into the water
for fun.

We like this, they say.

---

new words

      into   We   we

Jump this, Pat, jump this, says Peter.

Jump in the water.

You can jump.

Pat jumps into the water.

no new words

Pat jumps.

He jumps into the water.

He likes to jump.

It is fun, says Jane,
we like this.

---

new word

to

We have to go, says Peter.

Come, Jane.
Come, he says.
We have to go.

---

new word

go

We have to go, Pat,
says Jane.
Come, Pat, come.

Yes, says Peter,
we have to go.

---

new word

Yes   yes

Can we have some sweets?
says Jane.

Can we go to the shop
for some sweets?

Yes, says Peter.

---

new word

sweets

This is the shop, Jane.

Yes, this is it.

They have sweets and toys.

We want sweets, says Jane.

no new words

Peter and Jane go into the sweet shop.

Pat is in the shop.

Jane and Peter have some sweets.

Pat has a sweet.

---

no new words

I want to go home,
says Jane.

Yes, I want to go home,
says Peter.

Come, Pat, come.

We want to go home.

---

new word

home

Here we are, says Jane.
We are home.
It is fun in the water.

Yes, says Peter,
we have fun in the water.

no new words

New words used in this book

Page			Page		
4	Pat		28	—	
6	they	are	30	can	jump
8	water	fun	32	into	we
10	come	it	34	—	
12	says		36	to	
14	have	he	38	go	
16	look		40	yes	
18	fish		42	sweets	
20	wants		44	—	
22	no	you	46	—	
24	some		48	home	
26	for	this	50	—	

Total number of new words 27